Reader Level
Breakthrough
———
Unique Characters
150

I0686011

花马

Huā Mǎ

In Search of Hua Ma

John Pasden and Jared Turner

Mandarin Companion

Chinese Graded Readers

Published by Mind Spark Press LLC Shanghai, China

Mandarin Companion is a trademark of Mind Spark Press LLC.

Copyright © Mind Spark Press LLC, 2019

For information about educational or bulk purchases, please contact Mind Spark Press at BUSINESS@MANDARINCOMPANION.COM.

Instructor and learner resources and traditional Chinese editions of the Mandarin Companion series are available at WWW.MANDARINCOMPANION.COM.

First paperback print edition 2019

Library of Congress Cataloging-in-Publication Data In Search of Hua Ma: Mandarin Companion Graded Readers: Breakthrough Level, Simplified Chinese Edition / John Pasden and Jared Turner; [edited by] John Pasden, Chen Shishuang, Li Jiong, Ma Lihua Shanghai, China: Mind Spark Press LLC, 2019 Library of Congress Control Number: 2019948191

ISBN: 9781941875537 (Paperback)
ISBN: 9781941875551 (Paperback/traditional ch)
ISBN: 9781941875544 (ebook)
ISBN: 9781941875568 (ebook/traditional ch)

MCID: SFH20220804T194737

What Graded Readers can do for you

Welcome to Mandarin Companion!

We've worked hard to create enjoyable stories that can help you build confidence and competence and get better at Chinese–at the right level for you.

Our graded readers have controlled and simplified language that allows you to bring together the language you've learned so far and absorb how words work naturally together. Research suggests that learners need to "encounter" a word 10-30 times before truly learning it. Graded readers provide the repetition that you need to develop fluency NOW at your level.

In the next section, you can take an assessment and discover if this is the right level for you. We also explain how it won't just improve your Chinese skills but will have a wide range of benefits, from better test scores to increased confidence.

We hope you enjoy our books, and best of luck with your studies. Jared and John

Frequently Asked Questions

Do you have versions with pinyin over the characters?

No. Although this method is common for native Chinese learners, research and experience show it distracts a second language learner and slows down their ability to learn the characters. If you require pinyin to read most of the characters at this level, you should read something easier.

Is there an English translation of the story?

No. Research and experience show that an English translation will slow down the development of your Chinese language learning skills.

Is this the right level for me?

Let's find out. Open to a story page with characters and start reading. Keep track of the number of characters you *don't* know but don't count any key words you don't know. If there are more than 5 unknown characters on that page, you may want to consider working on your basic character recognition before attempting a graded reader. If the unknown characters are fewer than 5, then this book is likely at your level! If you find that you know all the characters, you may be ready for a higher level. However, even if you know all the characters but are reading slowly, you should consider building reading speed before moving up a level.

How do you decide which characters to include at each level?

Each level includes a core set of characters based on our extensive analysis of the most common characters and words taught to and used by those learning Chinese as a second language. All books at each level are based on the same core set and they can be read in any order.

What to expect in a Breakthrough book?

It's important that you read at the level that is right for you. Check out the next page to learn more about Extensive Reading and how we use that in graded readers to support the learning of Chinese by just enjoying a good story.

Books in our Breakthrough Level like this one:

- Include a core set of 150 Chinese words and characters learners are most likely to know.
- Are about 5,000 characters in length
- Use level appropriate grammar

- Include pinyin and a translation of words and characters you are not expected to know at this level
- Include a glossary at the back of book
- Include proper nouns that are underlined

What is Extensive Reading?

It will improve test scores, your reading speed and comprehension, speaking, listening and writing skills. You'll pick up grammar naturally, you'll begin understanding in Chinese, your confidence will improve, and you'll enjoy learning the language.

Graded Readers are based on science that is backed by mountains of research and proven by learners all over the world. They are founded on the theories of Extensive Reading and Comprehensible Input.

Extensive Reading is reading at a level where you can understand almost all of what you are reading (ideally 98%) at a comfortable speed, as opposed to stumbling through dense paragraphs word by word.

When you read extensively, you'll understand most of the words and find yourself fully engaged with the story.

Reading at 98% comprehension is the sweet spot to max out your learning gains. You do still learn at the Intensive Reading level (90–98%), but the closer you are to the Extensive level, the faster your progress.

No one should be reading below a 90% comprehension level.

It's called Reading Pain for a reason. You spend so much time in a dictionary and after 30 painful minutes on ONE paragraph, you're not even sure what you've just read!

If you want to know more, check out our website

www.mandarincompanion.com

Table of Contents

Story Notes

The Mandarin Companion 150-character Breakthrough Level empowers Chinese learners to begin with positive and enjoyable experiences reading Chinese. For learners at this level, reading a book in Chinese provides both a boost in fluency and a sense of accomplishment. Differing from higher level stories in the series, these are original stories co-written by John Pasden and Jared Turner, specifically designed to engage readers despite the limitations.

Stories at the Breakthrough Level are unique, with all books limited to the same small set of 150 characters comprising nouns, verbs and adjectives repeated throughout the books. Keywords are selectively borrowed from within the Mandarin Companion Level 1 standard. Those who can read this book at an enjoyable pace are already well on their way towards reading Mandarin Companion Level 1 stories.

In Search of Hua Ma is one of our more fantastical stories, partly inspired by books like *Alice in Wonderland* and *The Lion, the Witch, and the Wardrobe*. However, this story also ties into the larger "Mandarin Companion Universe." Continue reading other Mandarin Companion stories and you'll find a character from this story in *The 60-Year Dream*, a Mandarin Companion Level 1 story.

Character Adaptations

The following is a list of the characters from this Chinese story followed by their corresponding English names from John Pasden and Jared Turner's original story. The names below are not translations; they are new Chinese names used for the Chinese versions of the original characters. Think of them as all-new characters in a Chinese story.

南南 (Nánnán) – Nannan
妈妈 (Nánnán Māma) – Nannan's Mom
老太太 (Lǎo Tàitai) – Old Woman
老头 (Lǎotóu) – Old Man
花马 (Huā Mǎ) – Hua Ma

Cast of Characters

南南
(Nánnán)

妈妈
(Nánnán Māma)

老太太
(Lǎo Tàitai)

老头
(Lǎotóu)

花马
(Huā Mǎ)

RUSSIA

• Urumqi

Locations

山西 (Shānxī)

Shanxi Province in northern China (not to be confused with Shaanxi 陕西), meaning "West of the Mountains", is characterized by arid plateaus surrounded by mountain ranges.

海南 (Hǎinán)

The southernmost province of China, Hainan is a large tropical island off the southern coast of mainland China. Today it is known as a popular tourist destination for its clear water and white sandy beaches.

• Lhasa

MYANMAR

MONGOLIA

Shenyang

NORTH KOREA

Beijing
☆

Tianjin

Dalian

SOUTH KOREA

山西 Shanxi

Qingdao

Yellow Sea

Xi'an

Nanjing
Suzhou

Shanghai
Ningbo

Chengdu

Wuhan

Hangzhou

East China Sea

Taiwan

Guangzhou

Hong Kong

Macao

South China Sea

VIETNAM

LAOS

海南 Hainan

THAILAND

PHILIPPINES

去山上找花

　　山西有很多山，很多山西人都<u>住在</u>₁<u>山上</u>₂。南南和他的爸爸妈妈也<u>住在</u>₁山西的一个<u>山上</u>₂。

　　南南每天都去<u>山上</u>₂玩，<u>因为</u>₃<u>山上</u>₂有很多很<u>好玩</u>₄的<u>地方</u>₅。<u>山上</u>₂也有<u>一些</u>₆花，<u>可是</u>₇都很小，也不是很<u>好看</u>₈。

1　住在 (zhù zài) *vc.* to live (in/at)
2　山上 (shānshàng) *phrase* on the mountain(s)
3　因为 (yīnwèi) *conj.* because
4　好玩 (hǎowán) *adj.* fun

5　地方 (dìfang) *n.* place
6　一些 (yìxiē) *n.* some
7　可是 (kěshì) *conj.* but
8　好看 (hǎokàn) *adj.* good-looking

山上的人没有很多钱，可是，大家

还是很开心。

一天早上，南南听爸爸说，妈妈

的生日快到了。他很开心，他要在妈

9　大家 (dàjiā) *n.* everyone

10　还是 (háishi) *conj., adv.* still

11　开心 (kāixīn) *adj.* happy

12　早上 (zǎoshang) *tn.* morning

13　听 (tīng) *v.* to listen (to)

14　生日 (shēngrì) *n.* birthday

妈生日那天给她一个东西。因为每年
南南生日的时候，妈妈都有东西给他。
那些东西都不用花很多钱，可是，南
南很开心。

南南想："我给妈妈什么东西呢？"
他没有钱。他要的东西，爸爸妈妈会
给他。可是，他们不会给他钱。

"怎么做呢？什么东西又好看，又
不花钱？"南南在山上一边走，一边看。

---

15 那天 (nà tiān) *tn.* that day
16 东西 (dōngxi) *n.* thing(s), stuff
17 每年 (měi nián) *phrase* every year
18 的时候 (de shíhou) *phrase* when…
19 怎么 (zěnme) *adv.* how

20 又 (yòu) *adv.* again
21 花钱 (huā qián) *vo.* to spend money
22 一边 (yībiān) *conj.* while doing… (two things)

"有了!"南南开心地说。
₂₃

回到家，妈妈问："南南，你怎么
₂₄　　　　　　　　　　　₁₉

这么开心?"
₂₅　₁₁

"这个还不能说。可是，你会知道
₂₆　　　　　　₇

的。"南南开心地说。
₂₃

---

23 开心地 (kāixīn de) *phrase* happily   26 还 (hái) *adv.* still
24 家 (jiā) *n.* home   27 第二天 (dì-èr tiān) *phrase* the next day
25 这么 (zhème) *adv.* so⋯

第二天,南南一个人去山上找花。山

上的花不多，南南一个人找了很长时

间，还是没找到很好看的花。

不知道走了多长时间，南南看到

了一个小房子。这个地方他没来过。

"这个房子这么老,谁会住在这个地

方呢?"

---

28 一个人 (yī gè rén) *phrase* alone
29 找 (zhǎo) *v.* to look for
30 时间 (shíjiān) *n.* time

31 多长时间 (duō cháng shíjiān) *phrase* how long (of a time)
32 看到 (kàndào) *vc.* to see
33 房子 (fángzi) *n.* house

看见了一个老太太

南南走到门边问："里面有人吗？"

没有人给他开门。南南看到门没有

关，开门走了进去。

"你找谁？"一个很老的老太太走

出来对南南说。

"老太太，你好，我叫南南。我在山

---

34 门边 (mén biān) *phrase* by the door

35 里面 (lǐmiàn) *n.* inside

36 开门 (kāimén) *vo.* to open the door

37 进去 (jìnqu) *vc.* to go in

38 老太太 (lǎotàitai) *n.* old lady

39 走出来 (zǒu chūlai) *vc.* to walk out (from)

40 叫 (jiào) *v.* to be called, to call; to tell (someone to do something)

上走了很长时间，不知道怎么走到了

这里，也不知道要怎么回家。"

"你为什么在山上走很长时间？你

要找什么？"老太太问。

"又大又好看的 花。明天是妈妈

回家 (huíjiā) *vo.* to go home

的生日，可是，我没有钱。只能来山
上找花。"南南看看老太太，又说："我
每天都去山上玩，我知道山上有一些
小花，可是，我找不到又大又好看的
花。"

"南南，你说你每天都去山上玩。你
在山上有没有见过'花马'"? 老太太
问。

"什么'马'?"南南问。

"'花马'。"老太太又说了一次。

---

42 只能 (zhǐnéng) *adv.* can only
43 看看 (kànkan) *v.* to take a look
44 找不到 (zhǎo bu dào) *vc.* to be unable to find

45 见过 (jiàn guo) *phrase* have met before
46 一次 (yīcì) *phrase* one time

"我不知道你说的是什么马。"南南说,"可是,我在山上没见过马。"

"我要你去找'花马'。"

"可是,我都说了,山上什么马都没有。"南南想老太太没听见。

"南南,要是找不到'花马',你不能回家。"老太太笑了笑,"要是你找到了,你可以回家,我也会给你又大又好看的花。"

"我要回家!因为明天是我妈妈

---

47 听见 (tīngjiàn) *vc.* to hear

48 要是 (yàoshi) *conj.* if

49 笑 (xiào) *v.* to laugh, to smile

的生日，我没有时间找你的马。"南
    14   30 29

南一边说，一边走出老太太的家。
  22   22   50   38   24

---

50 走出 (zǒuchū) *vc.* to walk out

Three

到海南了？

"这是什么地方……?" 南南出门以
后，看到了大海。

"这是哪儿？怎么会有大海？那些
山去哪儿了？我在哪儿?" 南南不知
道问谁，因为他一个人也看不到。

"这不是真的吧，我在哪儿……"

---

51 出门 (chūmén) *vo.* to go out the door, to go outside

52 以后 (yǐhòu) *adv.* after; later, in the future

53 大海 (dàhǎi) *n.* the ocean

54 怎么会 (zěnme huì) *phrase* how could

55 看不到 (kàn bu dào) *vc.* to be unable to see

56 真的 (zhēn de) *adj., adv.* real; really

他回头去开老太太家的门，可是，老
太太的家和那个老太太都不见了。

"怎么会这样……"南南很怕，他不
知道这是哪儿，他也不知道怎么做。

他在海边一边走，一边看。他看到
地上的字：海南。

"我在海南?我怎么会从山西到了海
南……"

"这里的海真好看!"南南看看大海，

---

57 回头 (huítóu) *vo.* to turn one's head   **60** 怕 (pà) *v.* to be afraid (of)

58 不见了 (bùjiàn le) *phrase* disappeared   **61** 海边 (hǎibiān) *n.* seaside

59 这样 (zhèyàng) *pr.* like this   **62** 地上 (dìshang) *n.* on the ground

这是他第一次看到这么好看的海。
　　　63　　32　　25　　8

南南从小到大都在山西。他没有去
　　　　64

过山西外面的地方。
　　　65　　5

海南的 天、大海都 很好看。可是,
　　　　　53　　8　　7

明天是妈妈的生日，南南要回山西的家。

"花马，花马，你在哪儿？"南南一边走，一边叫。南南想："'花马'是马的名字吗？"

南南想："老太太说我要去找她的马。可是，她也不说怎么找，我也不知道怎么找。"

在海边又走了一会儿，南南还是没有看到马。

---

66 名字 (míngzi) n. name　　　67 一会儿 (yīhuìr) tn. a little while

他不走了，对大海大叫："花马，你
在哪儿？花马，我是南南，我是来找
你的，你出来吧，跟我回家吧……"

说到这里，南南不说了，他想：花
马是马，马怎么可能知道有人在找它
……

这时候，他听到有人在说话。他看
到了他们，那些人看起来很小，都没
有南南大。

---

68 大叫 (dà jiào) *v.* to call out loudly

69 出来 (chūlai) *vc.* to come out

70 可能 (kěnéng) *adv.; aux* maybe, possibly; possible

71 这时候 (zhè shíhou) *phrase* at this time

72 听到 (tīngdào) *vc.* to hear

73 说话 (shuōhuà) *vo.* to speak (words), to talk

74 看起来 (kàn qǐlai) *vc.* to look...

找花马

"你们好。"南南说,"我<u>叫</u>南南,这

里<u>真的</u>是海南吗?你们是海南人吗?

你们在这里做什么?"

"对,我们是海南人。我们是这里

的<u>工人</u>。"一个人说。

"我是从山西来的。"南南说,"你

们这里有马吗?我是来<u>找马</u>的。"

"你要找什么马?"一个工人问。

"我今天在山上见到一个老太太,老太太说我找一个'花马'。"

"我们这里只有花,没有马。"一个工人笑了,"你看,那边有很多又

那边 (nàbiān) *n.* over there

大又好看的花。”

南南看了一下：“真好看！我也在给我妈妈找花！可是，我要找的是‘花马’，有人听说过它的名字吗？”

听他说完，大家都笑了。可是，他们只笑，不说。

南南说：“我从小到大都没见过马，你们见过吗？”

“你为什么要找‘花马’？你是马妈妈吗？”一个工人问。大家听了以后

77　一下 (yīxià) *adv.* briefly, for a second
78　听说 (tīngshuō) *v.* to hear tell, to hear said (that)
79　说完 (shuō wán) *vc.* to finish speaking

都在笑。

"什么马妈妈?"南南有一点生气了。"'花马'是马,对吗?我怎么会是它的妈妈?"

"你看,这里都是海,你要找的马会不会在海里呢?"一个人问南南。

大家还在笑。

南南看看海,又看看这些人,有一点生气地说:"马怎么可能住在海里?"

"谁说海里没有马?"一个工人

---

80 有一点 (yǒu yīdiǎn) *phrase* to be a little (too)

81 生气 (shēngqì) *vo., adj.* to get angry; angry

82 生气地 (shēngqì de) *phrase* angrily

有一点生气，大叫，"你没听说过海马

吗?"

大家又笑。

"海马是海马，不是我要找的马。

我要找真的马!"南南也大叫。南南

又说："我看，你们都不知道'花马'。好吧，我一个人去找。这个地方这么大，我要怎么走呢？"

"你看，那边有个小房子。"一个好心的工人说，"去那边吧。"

"谢谢。"南南对工人们说，"我走了。再见。"

84　好心的 (hǎoxīn de) *adj.* kind-hearted

头上有花的马

海南每个地方都有很多好看的花。

南南一边走一边看花。

"那是什么？"南南看到一个很大的东西。可是，他看不到它的头。

南南小心地走了过去："花马?！"

他大叫，"是你吗，花马？你是花马，对不对？"

---

85 小心地 (xiǎoxīn de) *phrase* carefully   86 过去 (guòqu) *vc.* to go over

南南很开心，因为这是马，它头
上还有一个很大的"花"字。

马看看南南，点了一下头。

"太好了！我找到了！我找到花马
了！"南南说，"花马，你知道不知道

---

87 点了一下头 (diǎn le yīxià tóu) *phrase* to
nod briefly

有人在找你，跟我回家吧。"

马点了一下头，跟南南走了。

"花马，我真怕找不到你。"南南笑

了一下，他很开心地说："你知道我

在找你，对不对？"

马点了一下头。

"你真是好马！回家以后，我们一

起去山上玩，好不好？"

马又点了一下头，可是，它不跟南

南走了。

---

88 一起 (yīqǐ) *adv.* together

"不对，花马，不是那边，是这边。

跟我走，好不好？"南南大叫。

马点了一下头，可是，它还是不听

南南的话，也不跟他走。

老人

"花马，你怎么了？怎么又对我点
____89____   __19__20__

头，又不听我的话呢？"南南看起来
__90__ __20__ __13__   __74__

有一点生气。
__80__   __81__

马又对南南点了一下头。
 __20__   __87__

南南想："花马怎么会这样？我说
                       __54__   __59__

什么它都点头，这不对吧……它是真
          __90__

的花马吗……？"
__56__

---

89 怎么了 (zěnme le) *phrase* what   90 点头 (diǎntóu) *vo.* to nod one's head
happened, what's the matter

马看了看大海，走了。

"花马，你去哪儿？这里是海南，我们的家在山西。跟我走吧。"南南一边走一边说。可是，马不跟南南走，南南也不知道怎么做，他想了想，跟马走了。

马走到一个小房子门边，不走了。

"花马，这是哪儿？"南南走到门边问："有人吗？"

开门的是一个很老很老的老头。他

---

91 想了想 (xiǎng le xiǎng) *phrase* thought about it for a second

92 老头 (lǎotóu) *n.* old man

问南南：“你找谁？”
₂₉

南南看了看说：“老先生，你好。
₉₃

我叫南南，我是跟花马来你家的。”南
₄₀   ₂₄

南问老人，“这是你的马吧？”
₉₄

---

93 老先生 (lǎo xiānsheng) *phrase* elderly gentleman

94 老人 (lǎorén) *n.* old person, old man

老头说："什么花马？我不知道这

是谁的马。"

南南说："老先生，你家里还有人

吗？我来问问你家人吧，他们可能

知道花马是谁的。"

"家人？这里只有我。你知道我是

谁吗？"老人问。

南南说："不知道。你叫什么？。"

"我叫什么……问得好，我也不知

道我叫什么。"

---

95 家人 (jiārén) *n.* family member(s)

96 问得好 (wèn de hǎo) *phrase* good question (lit. "well asked")

"老先生，花马来找你，你真的不知
道花马吗？"南南又问，"它来找你，可
能因为你们是朋友。"

老头说："我一个人住在这里，没
有朋友。"

"不会吧？你在这里住了多长时间₃₁了？"南南又问。₂₀

"我不知道。你不要问我了，我什么都不知道。你走吧。"老人要关门₉₄了。₉₇

---

97 关门 (guānmén) *vo.* to close a door

老人知道了

南南说："老先生，你不要关门。
你听我说完，可以吗?"

老人看看南南说："好吧，你进来
吧。"

南南说:"在山西的一个山上，有一
个老太太，跟你一样老。她叫我来找
花马。我找到了这个马，它头上也有

一个'花'字。可是，我也不知道它是不是花马。"

"那你问问这个马。"老人说。他笑了一下。

"我问过了，可是我问什么，它都会点头，我怎么知道是不是真的……"南南说完，看看马，问："花马，这个老人是你的朋友吗？"

马看看老人，点了一下头。

南南看看马，又问："花马，你头上的'花'字是这个老人写的吗？"

马看看老人，又点了一下头，大叫
了一下。

南南听了有一点怕，因为他想这马
只会点头。

"看起来，这马不是只会点头。"

老人笑了。

南南看老人笑了，又不怕了。南南

问："老先生，是真的吗？这个'花'

字是你写的吗？"

老人没听南南说话,他一边看马,一

边说："花，马，花，马，花……"

南南不知道老人怎么了,只能问马:"花

马，你知道吗？你真的知道我在问什

么吗？"

马没点头，也没叫。

这时候，老人笑了："不对，它不

是花马，花马不是马。"

"什么？你说什么？"南南说，"你再
说一次……"
₄₆

"花马是我，不是它。"老人又说。
₉₄ ₂₀

南南说："可是，你是人，你不
₇
是马。花马怎么会是人……你说的不
₅₄
是真的！"
₅₆

---

100 再 (zài) *adv.* again (in the future)

真的花马

"我说的是真的。'花马'真的是我的名字，不是马的名字。"老人看看马，笑了一下。

南南说："怎么会这样……那，这马是不是你的马?"

老头说："是我的马。"

"那，马头上的这个'花'字，也

是你写的?"南南开心地问。

"对。我在它头上写这个'花'字,因为我的名字是花马。"老人很开心,因为他知道自己是谁了, 他还找到了他的马。"你知道吗? 这马也很老了, 它没有我老, 可是, 我们是真的老朋友了。"

马点了一下头。

"真好!"南南开心地说,"我太开心了! 我找到了你, 你找到了你的老

朋友。我们可以回去了！老太太见到
　　　　　　　101　　　　　38

你，会很开心的！"
　　　　11

　　"什么老太太？"老人问，"她是谁？
　　　38　　　　　94

为什么她见到我会开心？"
　　　　　　　　11

　　"我也不知道那个老太太是谁，我
　　　　　　　　　　　38

---

101 回去 (huíqu) *vc.* to go back

和她也是第一次见面。她住在山上一

个很老的房子里。"

"那，我们去她家看看吧，可能我

知道她是谁。"老人说。

"可是，我也不知道我们要怎么

回去……出了她的家以后，我看到的

是大海，山都没了……我不知道我在

哪儿，我回头看的时候，老太太的家

不见了，她也不见了。"

---

102 见面 (jiànmiàn) *vo.* to meet

"那,我们能不能一起回去找一找?"
老人问。

"可以, 我知道那个地方的地上写了'海南'。那里可能有门。跟我走吧!"南南说。

"还有你。"南南看了看马。

马点了一下头，老人和南南一起笑了笑。

回山西

"我们到了!"南南很开心,"可是那个门,在哪里?"

老人说:"我知道这个地方。"

南南说:"门呢?"

老人笑了笑说:"你看,这不是门吗?"

南南看了看,真的有门了。"有门

了！怎么会?"南南说。真的是老太太

家的门。

"太好了，那我们进去看看吧。"老

人对南南笑笑。马也点了一下头。

南南有一点怕，"我要回家，我要回

家！可是，这样能回去吗?"

"你不进去也可以，你要一个人在

这里吗?"老人笑了笑问。

"我不要一个人在这里……"南南

叫，"我还是跟 你 们一起进去吧。"

说完，老人开了门，他们一起进去了。

他们看到了老太太。南南开心地说："花马，你看！是那个老太太，我们回来了！"

"花马，是你吗？他真的找到你了！"

老太太看到老人和马，开心地笑了笑。她走过来，说："花马，你回家了。"

"是我，我回来了。对不起，我不会再走了。"

---

103 回来 (huílai) *vc.* to come back
104 走过来 (zǒu guòlai) *vc.* to walk over
105 对不起 (duìbuqǐ) *phrase* I'm sorry

"你们是?"南南看看他们，问:"这

里是你们的家?"

"对，我们在这里一起住了很多年。"

老人说，"可是，我走了。我走了以后

我不知道我是谁，我在哪儿。现在我

知道了，我回来了。"

"一百年了……我们一百年没见面了……"老太太说。

"真的一百年了吗？对不起，我不会再走了。"花马说。

马点了一下头。

"老太太，我找到了花马，可以回家了吧？"南南问老太太。

"明天是你妈妈的生日，我说过我会给你一些又大又好看的花。"老太

太笑笑说，"你看，这些花都是给你

妈妈的。好看吗?"

"真好看!"南南笑了,"山西没有这

么好看的花。我在山上也没找到这么

好看的花。"

"谢谢你, 老太太。我回家了。"南南一边说一边走, 走到门边, 看了看老太太, 又说"这是我回家的门吗?"

"是回家的门, 南南。谢谢你! 再见。"老太太说完, 关上了门。

南南出了门, 又回头看了看老太太的家。可是, 老太太的房子……又不见了!

可是, 他看到了很多山, 他知道山上有他的家。

妈妈很开心

"爸爸妈妈，我回来了！"回到家，南南很开心。
₁₀₃ ₂₄ ₁₁

"南南，你去哪儿了？怎么这么开心？"妈妈一边和南南说话，一边做明天生日的饭。
₁₉ ₂₅ ₁₁ ₂₂ ₇₃ ₂₂ ₁₄

"妈妈，我有好东西要给你。"南南笑笑说。
₁₆ ₄₉ ₄₉

"什么好东西？"妈妈也笑。

"你看！"南南说，手里都是花。"爸爸，你也过来看看。"

"这么大的花?! 山上有吗？你在哪儿找到的？"爸爸问。"真好看！"

南南没说话，只笑了一下，说："妈妈，明天是你的生日，这些花是给你的。你开心吗？"

"谢谢儿子，妈妈很开心。"妈妈笑得很好看。

---

107 手里 (shǒu lǐ) *phrase* in one's hand
108 过来 (guòlai) *vc.* to come over

109 儿子 (érzi) *n.* son

"妈妈，看到你这么开心，我也很开
心。"南南说。

"儿子，我从小到大都没见过这么
好看的花。"

妈妈看看花，又问："南南，妈妈知
道，我们这里没有这么好看的山花。

妈妈要问你，这些花是哪里来的?"

"是一个朋友给我的。"南南有一点怕，爸爸妈妈都不知道他今天去找"花马"了。要是他们知道了，可能以后他都不可以再去山上玩了。

妈妈问:"这个朋友是老太太吗?"

南南说:"妈妈，你怎么知道?"

妈妈看了看爸爸，笑了。

Key Words 关键词 (Guānjiàncí)

1. 住在 zhù zài *vc.* to live (in/at)
2. 山上 shānshàng *phrase* on the mountain(s)
3. 因为 yīnwèi *conj.* because
4. 好玩 hǎowán *adj.* fun
5. 地方 dìfang *n.* place
6. 一些 yīxiē *n.* some
7. 可是 kěshì *conj.* but
8. 好看 hǎokàn *adj.* good-looking
9. 大家 dàjiā *n.* everyone
10. 还是 háishi *conj., adv.* still
11. 开心 kāixīn *adj.* happy
12. 早上 zǎoshang *tn.* morning
13. 听 tīng *v.* to listen (to)
14. 生日 shēngri *n.* birthday
15. 那天 nà tiān *tn.* that day
16. 东西 dōngxi *n.* thing(s), stuff
17. 每年 měi nián *phrase* every year
18. 的时候 de shíhou *phrase* when···
19. 怎么 zěnme *adv.* how
20. 又 yòu *adv.* again
21. 花钱 huā qián *vo.* to spend money
22. 一边 yībiān *conj.* while doing... (two things)
23. 开心地 kāixīn de *phrase* happily
24. 家 jiā *n.* home
25. 这么 zhème *adv.* so···
26. 还 hái *adv.* still

27. 第二天 dì-èr tiān *phrase* the next day
28. 一个人 yī gè rén *phrase* alone
29. 找 zhǎo *v.* to look for
30. 时间 shíjiān *n.* time
31. 多长时间 duō cháng shíjiān *phrase* how long (of a time)
32. 看到 kàndào *vc.* to see
33. 房子 fángzi *n.* house
34. 门边 mén biān *phrase* by the door
35. 里面 lǐmiàn *n.* inside
36. 开门 kāimén *vo.* to open the door
37. 进去 jìnqu *vc.* to go in
38. 老太太 lǎotàitai *n.* old lady
39. 走出来 zǒu chūlai *vc.* to walk out (from)
40. 叫 jiào *v.* to be called, to call; to tell (someone to do something)
41. 回家 huíjiā *vo.* to go home
42. 只能 zhǐnéng *adv.* can only
43. 看看 kànkan *v.* to take a look
44. 找不到 zhǎo bu dào *vc.* to be unable to find
45. 见过 jiàn guo *phrase* have met before
46. 一次 yīcì *phrase* one time
47. 听见 tīngjiàn *vc.* to hear
48. 要是 yàoshi *conj.* if
49. 笑 xiào *v.* to laugh, to smile
50. 走出 zǒuchū *vc.* to walk out
51. 出门 chūmén *vo.* to go out the door, to go outside
52. 以后 yǐhòu *adv.* after; later, in the future
53. 大海 dàhǎi *n.* the ocean
54. 怎么会 zěnme huì *phrase* how could
55. 看不到 kàn bu dào *vc.* to be unable to see
56. 真的 zhēn de *adj., adv.* real; really
57. 回头 huítóu *vo.* to turn one's head
58. 不见了 bùjiàn le *phrase* disappeared
59. 这样 zhèyàng *pr.* like this
60. 怕 pà *v.* to be afraid (of)
61. 海边 hǎibiān *n.* seaside

62. 地上 dìshang *n.* on the ground
63. 第一次 dì-yī cì *phrase* first time
64. 从小到大 cóng xiǎo dào dà *phrase* from a young age until adulthood
65. 外面 wàimian *n.* outside
66. 名字 míngzi *n.* name
67. 一会儿 yīhuìr *tn.* a little while
68. 大叫 dà jiào *v.* to call out loudly
69. 出来 chūlai *vc.* to come out
70. 可能 kěnéng *adv.; aux* maybe, possibly; possible
71. 这时候 zhè shíhou *phrase* at this time
72. 听到 tīngdào *vc.* to hear
73. 说话 shuōhuà *vo.* to speak (words), to talk
74. 看起来 kàn qǐlai *vc.* to look...
75. 工人 gōngrén *n.* worker
76. 那边 nàbiān *n.* over there
77. 一下 yīxià *adv.* briefly, for a second
78. 听说 tīngshuō *v.* to hear tell, to hear said (that)
79. 说完 shuō wán *vc.* to finish speaking
80. 有一点 yǒu yīdiǎn *phrase* to be a little (too)
81. 生气 shēngqì *vo., adj.* to get angry; angry
82. 生气地 shēngqì de *phrase* angrily
83. 海马 hǎimǎ *n.* seahorse
84. 好心的 hǎoxīn de *adj.* kind-hearted
85. 小心地 xiǎoxīn de *phrase* carefully
86. 过去 guòqu *vc.* to go over
87. 点了一下头 diǎn le yīxià tóu *phrase* to nod briefly
88. 一起 yīqǐ *adv.* together
89. 怎么了 zěnme le *phrase* what happened, what's the matter
90. 点头 diǎntóu *vo.* to nod one's head
91. 想了想 xiǎng le xiǎng *phrase* thought about it for a second
92. 老头 lǎotóu *n.* old man
93. 老先生 lǎo xiānsheng *phrase* elderly gentleman
94. 老人 lǎorén *n.* old person, old man
95. 家人 jiārén *n.* family member(s)
96. 问得好 wèn de hǎo *phrase* good question (lit. "well asked")

97. 关门 guānmén *vo.* to close a door
98. 进来 jìnlai *v.* to come in
99. 一样 yīyàng *n.* the same
100. 再 zài *adv.* again (in the future)
101. 回去 huíqu *vc.* to go back
102. 见面 jiànmiàn *vo.* to meet
103. 回来 huílai *vc.* to come back
104. 走过来 zǒu guòlai *vc.* to walk over
105. 对不起 duìbuqǐ *phrase* I'm sorry
106. 一百年 yībǎi nián *phrase* 100 years
107. 手里 shǒu lǐ *phrase* in one's hand
108. 过来 guòlai *vc.* to come over
109. 儿子 érzi *n.* son

Part of Speech Key

adj. Adjective	*prep.* Preposition
adv. Adverb	*pr.* Pronoun
aux. Auxiliary Verb	*pn.* Proper noun
conj. Conjunction	*tn.* Time Noun
cov. Coverb	*v.* Verb
mw. Measure word	*vc.* Verb plus complement
n. Noun	*vo.* Verb plus object
on. Onomatopoeia	
part. Particle	

Grammar Points

For learners new to reading Chinese, an understanding of grammar points can be extremely helpful for learners and teachers. The following is a list of the most challenging grammar points used in this graded reader.

These grammar points correspond to the Common European Framework of Reference for Languages (CEFR) level A2 or above. The full list with explanations and examples of each grammar point can be found on the Chinese Grammar Wiki, the definitive source of information on Chinese grammar online.

ENGLISH	CHINESE
CHAPTER 1	
Special cases of "zai" following verbs	Verb + 在 + Place
The "also" adverb "ye"	也 + Verb / Adj.
Cause and effect with "yinwei" and "suoyi"	因为……所以……
Expressing "when" with "de shihou"	……的时候
Expressing "together" with "yiqi"	一起 + Verb
Two words for "but"	……，可是 / 但是……
Degree complement	Verb + 得……
Questions with "ne"	……呢?
Expressing "both A and B" with "you"	又……又……
Simultaneous tasks with "yibian"	一边 + Verb 1 (,) 一边 + Verb 2
Ordinal numbers with "di"	第 + Number (+ Measure Word)

CHAPTER 6

Direction complement "-qilai"	Verb / Adj.+ 起来
Expressing "everything" with "shenme dou"	什么 + 都 / 也 ……

CHAPTER 7

Basic comparisons with "yiyang"	Noun 1 + 跟 / 和 + Noun 2 + 一样 + Adj.

CHAPTER 8

Expressing "excessively" with "tai"	太 + Adj. + 了

CHAPTER 9

Expressing "will" with "hui"	会 + Verb

Credits

Story Authors : John Pasden, Jared Turner
Editor-in-Chief : John Pasden
Content Editor : Chen Shishuang
Editors : Li Jiong, Ma Lihua
Illustrator : Hu Sheng
Producer : Jared Turner

Acknowledgments

We are grateful to Ma Lihua, Li Jiong, Song Shen, Tan Rong, Chen Shishuang, and the entire team at AllSet Learning for working on this project and contributing the perfect mix of talent to produce this series.

Special thanks to Wang Hui and her 7th grade Chinese dual immersion class at Adele C. Young Intermediate School for being our test readers: AJ Bushnell, Brandon Murray, Colin Grunander, Emma Page, Isaak Diehl, Jackson Faerber, Jason Lee, Kyden Cefalo, Max Norton, Maxwell Isaacson, Olivia Barker, and Xavier Putnam. Also thanks to Jake Liu, Paris Yamamoto, Rory O'Neill, and Miles Turner for being our test readers.

About Mandarin Companion

Mandarin Companion was started by Jared Turner and John Pasden, who met one fateful day on a bus in Shanghai when the only remaining seats forced them to sit next to each other.

John majored in Japanese in college in the US and later learned Mandarin before moving to China, where he was admitted into an all-Chinese masters program in applied linguistics at East China Normal University in Shanghai. John lives in Shanghai with his wife and children. John is the editor-in-chief at Mandarin Companion and ensures each story is written at the appropriate level.

Jared decided to move to China with his young family in search of career opportunities, despite having no Chinese language skills. When he learned about Extensive Reading and started using graded readers, his language skills exploded. In 3 months, he had read 10 graded readers and quickly became conversational in Chinese. Jared lives in the US with his wife and children. Jared runs the business operations and focuses on bringing stories to life.

John and Jared work with Chinese learners and teachers all over the world. They host a podcast, You Can Learn Chinese, where they discuss the struggles and joys of learning to speak the language. They are active on social media, where they share memes and stories about learning Chinese.

You can connect with them through the website
www.mandarincompanion.com

Other Stories from Mandarin Companion

Breakthrough Readers: 150 Characters

The Misadventures of Zhou Haisheng
《周海生》
by John Pasden, Jared Turner

My Teacher Is a Martian
《我的老师是火星人》
by John Pasden, Jared Turner

Xiao Ming, Boy Sherlock
《小明》
by John Pasden, Jared Turner

Just Friends?
《我们是朋友吗?》
by John Pasden, Jared Turner

Level 1 Readers: 300 Characters

The Secret Garden
《秘密花园》
by Frances Hodgson Burnett

The Sixty Year Dream
《六十年的梦》
by Washington Irving

The Monkey's Paw
《猴爪》
by W. W. Jacobs

The Country of the Blind
《盲人国》
by H. G. Wells

Sherlock Holmes and the Case of the Curly-Haired Company
《卷发公司的案子》
by Sir Arthur Conan Doyle

The Prince and the Pauper
《王子和穷孩子》
by Mark Twain

Emma
《安末》
by Jane Austen

The Ransom of Red Chief
《红猴的价格》
by O. Henry

Level 2 Readers: 450 Characters

Great Expectations: Part 1
《美好的前途（上）》
by Charles Dickens

Great Expectations: Part 2
《美好的前途（下）》
by Charles Dickens

Journey to the Center of the Earth
《地心游记》
by Jules Verne

Jekyll and Hyde
《江可和黑德》
by Robert Louis Stevenson

Mandarin companion is producing a growing library of graded readers for Chinese language learners.

Visit our website for the newest books available:

WWW.MANDARINCOMPANION.COM

www.ingramcontent.com/pod-product-compliance
Lightning Source LLC
Chambersburg PA
CBHW070752180626
46818CB00007B/3091